FriesenPress

Suite 300 - 990 Fort St
Victoria, BC, V8V 3K2
Canada

www.friesenpress.com

ISBN
978-1-5255-2431-8 (Hardcover)
978-1-5255-2432-5 (Paperback)
978-1-5255-2433-2 (eBook)

1. JUVENILE FICTION, FANTASY & MAGIC

Distributed to the trade by The Ingram Book Company

The Girl From the Bottom of the Sea

Imagined, Told and Written by

Anne Van Roon

Chapter 1
The Girl

It was noon. Mani was walking home on the dreary street and thinking about how nothing exciting ever happened in her life.

Even today at school, on Founder's Day, nothing exciting had happened. Instead of a great celebration to mark the 313th year of humans moving under the waves of the ocean to escape the poisoned land, there was only a boring reading of the First Events and the reciting of the list of Presidents Under the Waves. There was no food, no music, no beautiful clothes, nothing to mark this day as special.

Mani hoped every year that she would learn more about the Over, and about the reasons that people had had to move under the waves. Suddenly, she realized that she had never even seen a stranger here under the dome. Everyone was familiar and known and greeted by name. The only strangers she ever met were in the books that she could take out from the meager library at her school. The Over was rarely mentioned, except on anniversary dates, and never with any happiness. People of The Over were spoken of with something like a soft hatred. After all, their many deeds caused the death of The Over world, poisoned the water and the land, and forced people under the waves.

"Thank goodness for the domes," grownups would say with relief. Since there was no one alive that remembered the real Over world from before, there was nothing to miss. Instead, people clung to their quiet lives that consisted of work or school or rest, never looking for anything new or different.

As she walked, Mani looked at the great dome above her, sheltering her and her family and her neighbours from the ocean's weight. Her dome was a habitation and schooling dome; attached to it were four other domes: one was for greenhouses that grew food, one was for packaging the food to export to other dome clusters, one was for processing water and oxygen, one was for submarines and underwater ships, and the last was for the machinery that kept the domes running. All together, the cluster was called a 'pod.' And today, the light in the pod was as grey as always, just like the streets and the houses and even the clothes that everyone wore.

The damp of the domes was ever present, the moisture from the sea seeping in at the cracks and coloring the street corners and depressions with shiny, colorless puddles. The colors on the buildings were softened by age and wear, as if the under-dome inhabitants had run out of the bright reds and greens and blues and now resorted to the dull greys and dirty whites that were left over.

As she walked, Mani looked up at the dome, its exterior darkened by years of seawater and sludge that the cleaning bots were now unable to remove properly. Its darkened surface reflected the soft lights of the habitation dome very poorly, making even the day cycle seem like a long evening. And although the day lighting was brighter, and the night cycle dimmed to keep people on a regular sleep-wake pattern, there was never a time without some kind of light. It was like living in an endless, waking dream.

Mani herself was very quiet, as quiet as the softly humming street-lights. As quiet as the people that she saw as she walked, talking softly. As much as she wanted to shout and run, she wouldn't. The dome had a way of reflecting all the sounds back to a person so even a normal voice would sound too big for the space; even whispers in the wrong spot under the dome were heard in other places, so secrets were never told outside and often not at all.

Down the straight street Mani trudged, walking slowly past the handful of colorless trading shops and the small open space with a cluster of lonely benches and an abandoned table. This area was the habitation pod's social gathering spot, located right below the center of the top of this dome. In historic pictures of what was known as the Beginning of the Under Gathering, this space was bright, the benches a cheerful yellow and people in smiles and fresh clothing gathered together under some potted growing areas to celebrate the safe arrival of those chosen to live under the sea. Now the benches were faded to a dirty cream, their joints rusting, and the area abandoned as people quietly moved from work to home and vice versa. The shrubs and flowers had long ago died from lack of proper lighting, and the container areas were cleared away to make room for a few more shops.

As soon as she neared home, Mani realized something was amiss. The podlet that she occupied with her mother and her father was normally quiet and empty after her day at school, but today the front door was open. Her parents should not be done work yet, so there was no reason that the door should be open. Life under the dome was so safe and boring that there was never a worry about staying home alone until her Mother would return. Now, though, Mani felt a tingle of worry and decided to go to the podlet next door where her friend Emly lived. Emly's mother would always let her visit for as long as it took for one of Mani's parents to return from their day jobs.

Since Emly was her best friend, Mani found no shortage of fun things to do together at her house. Both girls loved to draw and do crafts, and they were creating a whole new world in their sketchbooks right now. They had decided to call it Looloo Land, and they had made up funny creatures and plants and silly houses. They even started a new page all about the funny people that would live there. Giggling like crazy, they colored and talked.

Mani had almost forgotten about her house and the open door when the speaker buzzed in the kitchen at Emly's house. She heard Emly's mother speaking in a low voice at first, and then calling out to her:

"Mani, your mother says that dinner is ready, and you should go home now," she said.

"Thanks, Mother Hano," Mani said, nervous now as she walked toward the door to leave. She hesitated there, her hand on the door knob, wondering again what was happening at her house.

'You would think I was scared to discover an adventure!' she scolded herself. 'Maybe something exciting is happening at home and I'm missing out!' And with that, she opened the door and hurried to her own podlet.

It was a shock to Mani when she entered her front living room and discovered a total stranger sitting on her parents' couch across from her mother and father.

"Hello, Mani," he said kindly, his eyes wrinkling up at the corners. He looked like her father, but he was taller and had darker skin and shocking white hair, something never seen under the dome.

"I'm your Uncle Jock!" he said, smiling.

Mani's mouth dropped open in surprise. All she could do was stand there and stare.

Chapter 2

The Great Escape

After Mani got over her shock at meeting the stranger, she politely excused herself to wash up for dinner. As she helped her mother set the table, she kept stealing glances at her new uncle and her father, who were deep in quiet conversation on the couch.

What could they be talking about? she thought. Nothing ever happens here!

Dinner was also quiet, with Mani's mother glancing at her father, and her father looking at his brother many times. Uncle Jock, however, was full of conversation and asked Mani a great many questions: what was she learning in school? Did she have a best friend? What was her favorite subject? Mani answered every question, and found herself talking to Uncle Jock as if she had always known him. Soon, she worked up the courage to ask him a few questions, most of which he did not really answer. He would instead ask her another one, and then another one. When dinner was finished, Mani helped her mother clean up the kitchen and then headed off to her bedroom to finish homework and spend some time drawing in her sketchbook.

Finally, when Mani was too tired to draw any more and the clock said 8 pm, she knew it was time to get ready for bed. She washed up and when her mother and father came to kiss her goodnight, she asked them the question that had been on her mind since dinner had finished.

"How long will Uncle Jock be staying with us?" she said.

Her mother was quiet for a moment. Then she replied, "He will be with us until he finishes the business he came to see about. However long that takes."

"What business is he here about?" asked Mani.

Again, her mother was silent. Then she said very quietly, and very slowly, "His business is his alone. We'llll try not to get involved. And that means that we shouldn't tell anyone else about his visit here, Mani. Do you understand? People don't need to know that we have a visitor and a stranger among us. They might start asking questions, and your father and I don't want to speak about him. There might be trouble."

"I understand," said Mani. But she didn't. How would she go to school tomorrow and not tell her friends? It would be so exciting! But the look on her mother's face was so serious that Mani nodded and told her that she would stay silent.

Suddenly, her mother kissed her and hugged her tight to her body, saying: "I love you very much, Mani, you know that, right?"

Surprised, Mani hugged her mother back just as tightly and said with great feeling, "Yes, of course I do Mama!" When her mother released her, Mani snuggled down into her quilt and let her mother tuck her in for the night. With one more kiss, her mother said goodnight, turned off the side lamp, and left, closing the door behind her with a firm click.

It was the middle of the night when Mani suddenly awoke. She could hear shouting in another room. It sounded like her parents and someone else. Running to her door, she opened it a tiny bit and looked across the hallway into her parents' room. There she saw Uncle Jock and her father, staring at each other and shouting as loud as she had ever heard anyone shout in the dome. It scared her, and her stomach started to flutter with fear. She could hear them arguing about secrets and trouble and people who were looking for Uncle Jock.

"You've brought trouble to my house!" shouted her father. "You should have stayed away. We're not ready to go back. She's too young to be exposed to these problems!"

"It's too late!" Uncle Jock shouted back, "I barely stayed ahead of them and they know where I ended up. There's no time left now! If you stay here you will be captured – or worse."

As Uncle Jock turned, he saw Mani through the crack in her door. He shouted in surprise, and Mani's mother came to the bedroom door as well and looked at her with fear on her face. She turned to her father and spoke urgently, "It's too late, Dida. You heard Jock. It's time that we stopped arguing and make haste. Get yourself together and let Jock help you get started."

With that, she strode across the hallway and opened Mani's door fully, turning on the light.

"Mani, listen carefully. You need to get dressed quickly and quietly, and I will bring you a packcase. You need to fill it with only what you need, only what you can fit in it. We must leave very quietly tonight, and as quickly as possible. You have 10 minutes."

Mani dressed so quickly that she buttoned up her sweater the wrong way twice. Before she could finish, her mother returned with a big yellow suitcase with four squeaky wheels. After she was dressed, she filled her suitcase with her favorite outfits, her sketchpad and drawing tools, her baby blanket that she slept with every night, and her treasured stuffy. Looking around her room, she tried to think of what it would be like to never sleep there again, in her bed, with her lamp, and her best friend next door.

"Hurry, Mani!" Her mother was at the door, motioning her to follow quickly. Mani realized that all of the lights were off in the house and her mother had a light orb clipped to her belt. In the hallway, her father had two packcases, one in each hand. As he walked hurriedly down the hall, Mani saw her uncle waiting, another light orb hanging from his hand. He motioned them all to pass through the door as fast as possible, out onto the street.

There, parked at the curb, was a strange vehicle that Mani had never seen; it looked like a large cart with a roof and four wheels, but it had no handle to pull it with. To her surprise, her uncle jumped into one of the four seats in the cart and her mother and father two of the others. Mani climbed awkwardly into the last open seat, clutching her packcase on her legs. With a quiet mutter the large cart lurchedforward, building up great speed as the they rode down one street onto another and then another. They passed from their dome into the adjoining one as fast as a lightning fish, then through it and into the next dome, then the next.

Mani had never even seen these domes. She stared at the scenes as they flew by, goggling at the machines, the tanks, and the greenhouses. And just as she was about to ask where they were going, they entered the last dome in the pod and came to a halt with a screech.

Once again, Mani's mouth hung open, because she saw something that had only ever been in a book for her: the top of a submarine sticking out of the pool of water in the huge dome!

Chapter 3

The Submarine

When you have grown up underwater, you know all about many of the machines and tools that are used to help you live there. You hear about submarines, and subaquatic domes, and oxygen generators and desalinators. Mani knew all about these things - from books. But she had never ever seen one, and she had never ever imagined that she would be getting into one.

As Uncle Jock parked the motorized vehicle, Mani noticed a man walking swiftly down the ramp from the submarine to greet them. He looked very worried and in a big hurry. Uncle Jock spoke rapidly to him and gestured toward Mani and her family, then to the submarine. Beside her, Mani's mother and father grabbed their suitcases and climbed quickly out of the cart, gesturing for to Mani to follow. And she did, as fast as her legs would carry her.

When all four of them had run up the ramp to the tower of the sub, Uncle Jock motioned for Mani to be the first one to climb down inside it. Her heart was beating like a drum in her chest, but she carefully swung over the top lip and clung to the rungs of the ladder that went down into the unknown parts of the sub. As she descended, she could hear sounds and see lights flashing; at the bottom of the ladder, she hopped off and turned to see a room swirling with people and filled with machinery, electronic noises and flashing consoles. After the dull grey of life under the dome, with its low humming and quiet conversations, this was a surprise for Mani. Who knew that so much stuff could be crammed into such a small space!

"Follow me," said Uncle Jock, who nodded at a door at one end of the room. "I will show you to the front of the sub, where you will be staying."

With that, he strode towards the door, opened it wide, and then stood to the side, waiting for Mani and her parents to follow him. To her surprise, her parents seemed to know exactly where to go. They did not hesitate once as they walked quickly past Uncle Jock into the passageway beyond. Mani lingeredin the door, peering into the engine room of the sub to take one last look at the amazing sight. As she did she heard Uncle Jock tell the crew that they needed to "dive with haste and get underway to the coordinates that were pre-arranged." The he pushed Mani through the doorway and hustled her down the hallway after her parents. Under her feet, Mani felt the submarine drop and the floor shift. She needed to hang onto the rail on the side wall to keep on her feet.

Even though life under the dome sometimes felt cramped and limited, it was nothing like life in this submarine. As Mani hurried to keep up with her parents and Uncle Jock, she had to constantly dodge other crew members, move around machines, or cross into other hallways. Down the hallway they went, then up some stairs, and then down some more, around a curve; it was confusing! One open doorway she passed let out the best smells of cooking and baking, and as she passed Mani looked in and saw a cafeteria, with people eating at tables. A large, jolly-looking woman was standing behind the counter in an apron. She smiled at Mani and waved as she passed by.

Suddenly, Mani and her parents passed through a part of the sub that was almost entirely made up of the same material as the dome back home. Mani could see through the curved walls into the dark ocean, the water swirling past as quickly as she felt the submarine moving. There was nothing to see in the darkness, but the feeling that they were now moving quickly was unmistakeable.

Finally, all of them followed Uncle Jock, now in the lead, into a final quiet passageway where he stopped in front of a door.

"This is your room, Mani," he said with a smile. "It's made for only one person, just cozy enough for you! And this one across the hall is for your parents." He gestured to the door across the hallway, where Mani's parents were already inside and putting their suitcases on the bed.

"Here are your things, Mani," said her mother, indicating her suitcase. "Why don't you go and get settled in your room? If you feel like lying down, now is the time to do it. We'll come and get you for some breakfast in a few hours."

Mani nodded and took her suitcase from her mother's hand and dragged it into her own room, shutting the door softly. She looked around. There was a small bed tucked against the wall, a porthole to look out into the sea, and a small sink on the opposite wall. With a sigh, she slid her suitcase under the bed, crawled on top of it, and settled with her head lying on the pillow. Underneath her, she could feel the submarine humming and whooshing through the water. It was soothing, and somehow familiar.

To her surprise, Mani fell dead asleep.

Chapter Four

A New Friend

Mani woke up slowly, her head fuzzy. She tried to remember where she was and what the humming and vibrating was all around her. Then she remembered everything suddenly and sat up, the events of the last day washing over her. What time was it? she wondered. She felt tired again and lay down on her back, staring at the ceiling of her little room.

A small tickling at her elbow had her glancing down at her arm, and to her amazement she saw a tiny head with two shiny black eyes and a round nose staring back at her! Mani didn't move, just kept staring at the little face, wondering what exactly this little creature was and how it came to be on a submarine.

As the creature sniffed her carefully and began to climb onto her arm, Mani could see that it looked a lot like a mouse or a rat, but instead of fur it had smooth skin and lots of short whiskers around its mouth. And gills! There were two rows of gills under each rounded ear. You could see them waving silently as the little animal explored Mani right up into her armpit. This amazing creature was all black except for a long thin stripe of white that started between its ears and ran all the way down to the end of its long, twitching tail.

As slowly as she could, Mani sat up and cupped the little animal in her right hand, careful not to scare it. It sat there, looking at her with a questioning face, waiting patiently.

"Well, I'm hungry, and I don't want to leave you here alone, so let me get my sweater on and let's go explore!" Mani told the adorable creature. As Mani got her sweater on and buttoned it up, she made sure to open the pocket on the front. Sure enough, the little thing jumped inside and curled up, ready to go.

Outside the small room, Mani made her way back down the hallway. She found her parents in the observatory part of the submarine, sitting and talking under the glasslike dome. When they saw her they opened their arms for a big hug, wrapping Mani up and squeezing her tight with all their love.

"Are you hungry?" Mani's mother asked. "We're about to go into the cafeteria and have breakfast."

"I'm starving!" Mani declared.

Smiling, her mother took her hand and they followed her father down the hallway yet again to the doorway that led into the eating area. Even before they got there, Mani's mouth was watering. She could smell bread, sugar, and something salty that was not anything like fish at all.

Once in the cafeteria, Mani's mother and father introduced her to the plump lady behind the counter. Her name was Cookie, and she wore a huge white apron and an even bigger, welcoming smile. As she gave Mani a tray of her own and showed her what was for breakfast, she kept smiling, winking at Mani once and laughing at a joke that her father was telling her. Mani had never met anyone as happy as Cookie, or as good a cook either. There were fresh buns, scrambled eggs, and something that was called bacon. That was Mani's favorite, and she ate five pieces.

When it was time to leave the cafeteria, Mani looked around to see that there weren't any other people watching, then approached Cookie slowly.

"Well hello again!" smiled Cookie, her eyes twinkling.

"Can I ask you something?" said Mani. "I'm not sure who else to ask."

"Go ahead, sweetheart!" laughed Cookie.

Mani checked to see that no one was watching her and then carefully opened her sweater pocket to show Cookie the little creature that was curled up in there.

"Do you know what this is?" asked Mani, looking worried.

Cookie gave a chuckle and put a gentle hand on Mani's shoulder. "Sweetie, that there is a sea snit. They like to hide on underwater boats and they can live in the water and above it too. Its real interesting that you have one there in your pocket because they are very shy and often hide away. They only approach a human if they have made a real connection with them and once they are your friend, they are your friend for life! They are extremely smart. They will guard you and keep you company and stay with you until they pass away. You must be real special, sweet pea, to have one come to you like this and choose you as a friend. You take care of it and share your food scraps with it, you hear? They eat people food, you know!" Cookie gave Mani another fresh bun and told her to keep it to share with her new friend.

"Have you given it a name yet?" asked Cookie.

"No," said Mani, "but I'd like to name it after my best friend from our dome, Em. What do you think?"

"That's a wonderful name, sweetheart," Cookie chuckled.

Mani gave Cookie a big hug, then ran down the hallway to her little room. Once she was there, she took out Em and stroked her soft skin, letting her tickle her hand with her whiskers.

"I'm going to take care of you always!" said Mani.

She had no idea how important this little friend was going to be for her in the next few weeks.

Chapter Five

The Over

Mani had been on the submarine for over three weeks now, and every day was very similar. She would wake up in the morning with Em snuggled into the crook of her neck, tickling her. When she got dressed, she would put Em into the pocket of her sweater and then head off to the cafeteria to see Cookie. Cookie was always waiting for Mani with a big smile and a special treat.

At breakfast each morning, Mani always chose bacon which made her very happy.

After breakfast, Mani would explore the open areas of the submarine. Uncle Jock often came to take her to special places, and after a while, the crew members recognized Mani and showed her even more interesting gadgets and machines. She could explore the engine room, the storage rooms, and even the glass observatory.

One day, Mani's parents came to her little room and told her that they needed to speak to her. As she followed them across the hallway to their room, she wondered what was going to happen. In their room she noticed that her parents had begun to repack their suitcases, and her stomach dropped in disappointment.

Suddenly, her mother turned to Mani, who was sitting on the bigger bed.

"Mani, we need to talk with you about something important. It's time for you to prepare yourself for a new experience. You see, we know that you have been taught in the school under the dome that The Over is not livable, and that the land is poisoned from the Great Wars. That is something that the Unders have chosen to believe because they don't want people to move away and empty out the domes.

"Sometimes the Unders believe that they are living in the only good place on Earth. But in truth, Mani, The Over is inhabited by many people, and your father and I used to live there before you were born. Some people didn't like the way we ran things, and they tried to kill us! We had to run and hide, and that was very difficult. We were very important people who made big decisions about how to run The Over. When we reach there, you will hear people refer to your father as the king, and to me as the queen. That means that you are a princess. We are the royal family there."

Mani was very quiet. She had thought that she would be living on the submarine with Uncle Jock, and since she was so small, she fit in the submarine just fine. Now she had found out that she was not only moving to another part of the world, but also into a brand new life that she knew nothing about.

Her mother continued, "Mani, we thought that we would be staying in The Under a lot longer, but when your Uncle Jock appeared suddenly, we knew that we needed to return. Most of the people that have wanted to get rid of us have been arrested and put in jail, but there are a few left who are hunting us down even as we speak. We need to stay ahead of them and get to a safe place where we can begin to work with the new government that is running The Over. You are going to be a part of that. You are going to meet many new people, and do many new things, and go to many new places. We hope you're ready for another adventure!"

Her mother gave Mani a huge hug, and even her dad came over to wrap his arms around both of them. Mani's heart was beating fast but she felt safe with her parents, and safer yet on her Uncle Jock's sub. Would that change now? She felt Em tickling her in her pocket as if she knew that Mani was upset, and thought about all the adventures that she would take her on now.

"How long until we get there?" asked Mani.

"Tomorrow!" said her mother, letting her out of the hug. "Do you think you're ready? You will love The Over, Mani. We do!"

Mani nodded. "Can I go see Cookie?" she asked. When she didn't know what to do, she would go and see Cookie, who would let her help in the kitchen and give her and Em a treat to share later. This always helped Mani think.

Her mother nodded, and Mani went off to the cafeteria. When she arrived, she could tell that Cookie already knew about her leaving. Her face looked sad but she put on one of her big smiles and gave Mani a hug and a cookie anyway. As Mani helped her set the dishes out for the supper sitting, Cookie told Mani that she would miss her very much.

"Maybe I can come back and visit you here?" said Mani, trying to be brave.

Cookie's face brightened up. "Of course, sweetie pie! You can always come and visit me here."

Then her face got serious and she looked right at Mani.

"I didn't want to forget to tell you, but you need to look after Em properly on The Over," she said, "You must let her get totally wet and under water at least once a day, okay? Fresh water or salt water, doesn't matter. Otherwise she will get very sick. Can you do that?"

Mani nodded. She patted Em in her pocket, and as she got ready to go pack her suitcase, Cookie gave her a small bag of treats to pack for her and Em, just in case. With a big last hug, Mani returned to her room.

The next day, Mani and her parents brought their suitcases back the way they had entered the submarine. It seemed like a lifetime ago that they had escaped the dome in the night, and here they were on the edge of another adventure. Mani felt the sub slowing down and finally stop as they were standing in the engine room, bumping into something and causing her to clutch at her mother.

A crewman climbed the ladder, turned the wheel, and popped the hatch on the turret. He climbed out and motioned to them to follow. This time Mani was last, and as she climbed out the top she was surprised that The Over was as grey and dreary as their dome. The sky was filled with grey clouds and she felt drops of water on her face.

As her eyes adjusted, she looked around in amazement at her surroundings. Unlike the old drab pictures in the books under the dome, the sky was indescribably huge. There was no sun showing at the moment, but across the sky the grey, metallic colored clouds were actually moving, sailing like living things. A strong breeze blew through her hair and whipped it past her face. Everywhere she looked, there was color: the stormy black sea, the masses of people and houses in every color that you could imagine, and thousands of plants Mani had never seen before.

Chapter 6

A New Place

Mani could hardly believe all the things that she was seeing with her eyes. After she climbed down the turret of the submarine onto the deck, she stood there, squinting in the falling rain. She was trying to look at all the colors and listen to all the sounds around her.

As she looked around, she saw Uncle Jock coming towards her with a colorful stick. He also had one of his own, only larger. She watched as he handed her the pink one, then took his dark blue one, pointed it away from him, and pressed a button with his thumb at the base of the stick. Instantly, it popped open into a dome of color, with the stick now holding it up like it was a flower on a stem. Mani copied Uncle Jock with her stick, holding it away from her, pressing the button, and watching with delight as it bloomed into a dome of pinks.

Uncle Jock chuckled at her surprised face. "It's an umbrella, Mani," he said. "Hold it over your head!"

Under their umbrellas, Uncle Jock and Mani followed her parents down the dock to another motorized car. This time, Mani could tell that her parents were leading and Uncle Jock was hanging back. It appeared her parents were now in their element; they seemed to know people and the people knew them! As she watched, people were bowing and taking off their hats, smiling and shaking hands with her father. Both of her parents were smiling with huge smiles, smiles that Mani had never seen before on them. As everyone climbed into the motorized black car, Mani heard someone yell, "It's good to have you back, Your Majesties!" The people all around murmured agreement.

The ride in the car was as exciting as the first time Mani had climbed down into the submarine. In the sky, the wind had blown the grey clouds off to the side of the horizon, and the bright sun was shining. Mani could feel the heat of the sudden sunshine on her, right through her sweater. She rolled down her window and looked at all the trees and birds and flowers, the houses and people and other strange animals passing by the window of her vehicle. Em in her pocket was stirring, probably – Mani assumed - smelling all the new smells and hearing the new sounds too.

As Mani watched, the car took a winding trip through the city, out into the forested area, and finally up around the large hill that Mani had seen from the dock. At the top of the hill she had seen a large building, something like a mansion or a castle from one of her under dome books. But as they drew nearer to the building Mani realized it was just a very large house, larger than any that she had seen in the city. There was a tall iron fence surrounding the land the house was on, and massive iron gates that swung open as they arrived. As they drove slowly up to the front of the estate, Mani noticed that it was on a beautiful white driveway lined with shells of every shape and color.

There were three people waiting at the open front doors to greet them as they climbed out of the car- two men and a slim woman with glasses and dark hair pulled into a bun. The two men smiled and shook her father's and uncle's hands, but the woman just pressed her lips together in a tight smile and stared down her nose at Mani.

"This is Mrs. Crank," said Uncle Jock to Mani. "She runs the house and looks after everything. If you ever need anything, or want to know anything, she can help you. Right, Mrs. Crank?" he looked at her expectantly.

Mrs. Crank twisted her mouth in a grimace, but she nodded her head yes. Mani looked at her face and wasn't sure that she would want to ask her for anything!

After a tour of the house and the many rooms, Mani was shown upstairs to her own bedroom, and saw that she was just down the hallway from her parents' bedroom as well. Uncle Jock told her that he was on the next level up, in the corner overlooking the garden. "It's the best spot in the house if there's a spot of trouble," he said quietly to Mani, and winked.

Once in her bedroom, Mani took her time examining all the beautiful items that she would be using. There was an ornately carved dresser, a large mirror on a stand, a bathroom that was bigger than three of the bathrooms on the submarine put together. The bed was fit for a king or a queen: huge, with fluffy covers and lacy pillows.

Mani took a moment and checked on Em, who was now sound asleep. Carefully, she removed her sweater and made a nest around Em on the end of the big bed. By now, Mani had realized that Em slept a lot, and that she liked to burrow in her sweater when she could, so Mani left her there to sleep and went off to explore the rest of the house.

Mani had never been in such a huge building. Even though the domes in The Under were huge, she didn't think of them as buildings, more like covers or ceilings. Here in the house there were endless rooms with interesting furniture, pictures on the walls, and objects and items that she had never seen before. And there were windows everywhere. Most were closed, but some were open, letting in the breeze and bringing in the soft perfumed smell of the outdoors and the sound of the many birds.

Mani soon found herself close to the kitchen. She could smell something cooking and hear the clatter of pots and pans. As she followed her ears down the smaller hallway, she found a large door that was open, and peered inside.

In the kitchen there were two ladies working on some sort of meal, and then there was Mrs. Crank, standing and stirring a pot on the stove. She was frowning and muttering to herself. Mani's stomach felt uneasy, and she felt the urge to leave right away. Out of the corner of her eye, she saw something dark go scurrying along the cupboard by Mrs. Crank. Em? she wondered. Maybe her eyes were playing tricks on her.

"What are you doing here?" Mrs. Crank suddenly shouted at Mani, scaring her half to death.

"I mean, what are you doing here, sweetie?" Mrs. Crank said with a fake smile pasted on. "Is there something I can do for you?" when she called Mani 'sweetie' it sounded wrong, nothing like when Cookie said it.

Mani was terrified, and stood there trembling. She was thirsty, but now she was too scared to ask for a drink. No one ever shouted under the dome. She had never had anyone shout at her in this way! Mani needed to get away from this lady as soon as possible.

"Um, I was looking for a drink? I'm thirsty." Mani stammered. She didn't want Mrs. Crank to think that she had been spying on her.

Mrs. Crank came over and gave her a glass full of yellow liquid and pieces of what looked like glass. "Here's some lemonade," she said, trying to sound sweet and kind. "Have as much as you want! It's made with lemons from our own lemon trees."

"What are lemons?" asked Mani, staring into the glass suspiciously.

Mrs. Crank gave her a funny look. "They are a yellow fruit. We use them to make drinks and sweets and cakes."

"Oh," said Mani, taking a sip of the sweet, tart drink. It tasted like sunshine and sugar, and the glassy pieces were ice! Mani had only seen ice in the food vendor's shop under the dome, but it was used to keep food cold, not in drinks. She finished the drink as quickly as she could, Mrs. Crank watching her like a hawk.

"Thank you," said Mani, remembering her manners at the last minute. Then she turned and hurried down the hallway as fast as she could. She suddenly felt the need to see Em and check on her parents.

Chapter 7
Trouble

Mani couldn't hurry down the hallway to her room fast enough after Mrs. Crank scared her. She rushed into her room and straight to the bed to check on Em. But Em wasn't there! Mani had noticed that sometimes Em would be gone for awhile and she wondered where she went.

Still worried, Mani put her sweater on and paced around her room. What could she do but wait now? Finally, she sat in the window seat and looked out onto the beautiful gardens. As she watched the breeze making the trees sway, and the birds flitting from tree to tree, she managed to relax, until there was a sudden knock on her door.

"Who's there?" she called.

"It's me, Mani," her mother replied. As she opened the door and came inside, Mani noticed that she was dressed in brand new clothing, a beautiful dress with gold stitching and a red sash that was draped across her chest. On her mother's head was a small tiara of diamonds that winked as she moved through the room towards Mani.

"It's time for dinner," her mother said, holding her hand out. "It's our first dinner together on The Over! Mrs. Crank has made some special dishes to celebrate our return from exile. I hope that you're hungry!"

"I am!" exclaimed Mani, her stomach growling suddenly in agreement. "Should I dress up too?" she asked her mother.

Her mother laughed. "No Mani, you don't have to start dressing up yet! This was mine before we left, and I have a whole royal collection of clothes waiting for me. You will have to visit the tailor to get fitted for your clothes and your sash. There is a small collection of jewellery for you that has been passed down through the years by the family, but we will look at them later. Right now, why don't we just go and eat together as a family?"

Mani felt better just being with her mother, so she nodded her head in agreement, and wondered for a moment what Mrs. Crank had made for supper. From the smells in the kitchen earlier, there was no bacon, and no sweet rolls like Cookie made on the submarine. It looked like supper here would be one more adventure.

The dining hall of the house was huge, with tall windows along one side that looked out onto the lawn and the forest beyond. Some of them were open, letting in the fragrant breeze. There was a long, polished table with settings for four at one endStanding at his setting was Uncle Jock, waiting patiently and smiling at Mani.

To her amazement, Mani saw that her table setting was made up of many different parts. Under the dome, setting the table meant that there was a plate or a bowl, a cup, and a fork, knife, or spoon. Here, in front of Mani, were a stack of three different plates topped by a bowl. On each side were four different kinds of cutlery, fancy golden ones that had curling vines on the handle and some initials. At the top of the setting were three things to drink out of: two crystal goblets and one metal mug, each with the same three initials on them, CVR. The three letters were intertwined, with the R being the largest letter, in the center, and the C and V on the left and right. As Mani sat down in her seat she watched her parents, copying them as they placed the napkin on their laps, chose cutlery, and had a drink. Occasionally, her father smiled at her and pointed to a fork or a knife during the dinner to demonstrate which one to use. Or Uncle Jock would nudge her elbow and wiggle his eyebrows as he took a bite of something in a dramatic fashion.

And what an elaborate dinner it was! There was a cold soup served by Mrs. Crank, who frowned and glowered at everyone. This was followed by a salad topped with strange flowers that tasted like honey. Mrs. Crank took Mani's away before she was done, serving the next part of the meal, some kind of pink meat with tiny potatoes. The meal went on for three more dishes, each one small and mysterious and delicious. Mani wasn't even full yet when Mrs. Crank brought in the dessert in crystal dishes, some kind of pink fluffy stuff with sprinkles and more exotic flowers. This time, Mrs. Crank was beaming a huge smile. It was a scary sight, making her pointed nose look even more pointed, and her teeth sharp and evil as well. She smiled widely as she placed a dessert in front of each person at the table, and then returned to the side door to stand and watch as everyone ate.

At that moment, Mani felt a tickle at her ankle, and a scrabbling up her leg into her sweater pocket. She knew it was Em. Em often came back from one of her outings and secretly climbed up into Mani's pocket to settle into another nap. Except this time, Em was rustling around frantically, poking her head out of the pocket to stare at Mani with a serious face and twitching whiskers.

Mani tried not to look obvious as she peered at Em, but Uncle Jock had seen her looking under the table and he raised his eyebrows at her in a silent question.

Mani straightened up and picked up her spoon, wanting to eat her beautiful dessert before Mrs. Crank took it away. In fact, her mother and father were almost finished theirs.

As soon as she tried to take a scoop of pink fluff, Em bit Mani on the arm. Mani jumped and dropped her spoon.

"Everything alright, sweetie?" her mother asked.

Mani nodded, picking up her spoon again. As she looked over, she saw that Mrs. Crank did not look happy that she was not eating. She was staring at her with a horrible look on her face.

Once again, Em bit her on the arm. This time Mani put the spoon down. She didn't want to get bitten, even if the dessert looked amazing. Beside her, Uncle Jock was watching quietly, his brows drawn together in concern. He took a deep breath and stood up out of his chair, his dessert also untouched.

"Please excuse me," he said. "I must attend to some paperwork in my study." He left the dining hall swiftly, looking back once at Mani with a serious face.

"May I be excused too?" Mani asked. "I would like to go rest in my room, and I am very full. The meal was very good." She looked at Mrs. Crank with her nasty face all screwed up in hatred, and left quickly as well, almost running up the stairs to her room.

To her surprise, Uncle Jock was waiting for her outside her door. He grabbed her arm and started walking her down the hallway and up the stairs to his private room and study. As they walked, he asked Mani in a stern voice, "Mani, do you have a snit in your pocket?"

Surprised, Mani nodded.

"Did it bite you when you tried to eat the dessert?" he asked.

Again, Mani nodded.

"Mani, I think that Mrs. Crank might have put something in the dessert to make us sick or put us to sleep. She must be working with our enemies. When I realized that you had a snit and that it was warning you, I knew I needed to get you out of here as fast as I could. You see, I had a snit when I was young and it would warn me when something was wrong by biting me. Your snit must have seen Mrs. Crank putting something in the dessert when it was sneaking around the house making sure everything was okay. That is what they do. Do you trust me, Mani? Can you be brave and follow me to a safe place? If our enemies can get you, then they can get your parents to do anything they want. I need to get you somewhere safe."

Mani nodded again as Uncle Jock rushed her into his study and through it to the bathroom. In the bathroom, he hustled her into his corner shower and closed the door when they were inside. Once the door was closed, he dialed the hot water dial backwards three times and pushed it in. The dial made a loud click.

Swiftly, the shower dropped down and down. Mani screamed in shock. She grabbed Uncle Jock's arm as the shower came to a stop and opened in an immense underground room. There were motorized vehicles everywhere, and Uncle Jock hurried her over to a gigantic one with massive tires. He helped her up inside, jumped into the driver's seat, and fired up the engine. With the push of a button a door opened at the end of the garage. Uncle Jock pushed hard on the accelerator, sending them shooting out of the garage and down a road into the deep forest.

As they raced away from the house Mani turned and looked back, searching for any sign of her parents, but there was none. It looked like it was just she, Em, and Uncle Jock who would be getting away.

Chapter 8

The Getaway

Uncle Jock drove the vehicle like a madman, swerving into the deep forest and bumping along the dirt road with a grim face. Twilight was falling and it was getting dark. Soon, he needed to turn on the massive truck's headlights so that they could continue the trip as quickly as possible.

At one point they emerged from the forest and Mani found that they were winding along a road that followed the edge of a high cliff. Below it, Mani could see the ocean in the night, churning and sparkling under the rising moon.

Even later, their journey took them away from the coastal road and onto a flat, open plain. There were no lights anywhere to be seen for a long time, except for the headlights on the big truck. Mani was growing sleepy until she noticed what looked like tiny lights ahead, ones that did not move. As time passed, they grew in number, and in size, getting bigger as Mani realized that they were drawing close. It looked to be a large city, one that was starting to spread out as they got closer.

Finally, they reached the outskirts of the city and Mani saw that the city was laid out in a large circle pattern, like a wagon wheel. The streets all led straight to the center of the city and then away from it as well. Not only that, but it seemed the city could only be entered through one gateway, an opening in what looked to be a volcanic rim that rose all the way around the rest of the city. The rim was higher at the opposite wall from the gateway, so tall in fact that Mani could no longer see any of the stars.

Driving slowly now, Uncle Jock made his way around a huge traffic circle, then straight ahead again, aiming toward the back of the high wall of the volcanic rim. It was late into the night. There was no one on the streets and all the houses and shops were dark and shuttered. Only the bright streetlights were shining. Mani thought they were watching like welcoming stars and keeping them on track to their destination, which suddenly appeared ahead, a surprise to Mani and an obvious relief to Uncle Jock.

It was a towering castle, many stories high, carved right out of the side of the volcano's inner rim. Even in the dark, Mani could see that it was at least ten stories tall.

Uncle Jock pushed another button in the truck and a great door opened to the side of the castle. He drove inside, following a long lighted tunnel down into another huge garage, filled with more vehicles.

As he parked, he turned to Mani and said with all seriousness, "Welcome to your true home, Mani. I didn't think that it would be under such terrible circumstances, but this is the family's main castle, the one that they rule from. Your parents and I were hoping that we would make our way here without incident, but you know that we needed to get away. When you come inside, there is someone very special that I want you to meet. I have already signalled ahead, and they are expecting us. Are you ready?"

Mani nodded, tired to the bone and worried about her parents. She was too worn-out to ask Uncle Jock about them, but he must have seen her anxious face because he added, "I'm sure your parents are not being hurt Mani. They are important people, and even their enemies would never do anything to harm them if they do what they are asked to. I promise you, I'm going to talk to our military right away and get some rescue plans into place as soon as possible!"

He took her hand and helped her out of the giant truck, and they made their way over to another door. It led into another elevator, but this one was very slow. There would be no screaming on this ride.

Once the doors opened, Mani could see into a massive open space lit with beautiful lamps. It was a circular room with lofty ceilings and an enormous spiral staircase that followed the outside of the room upwards. Opposite to the staircase was a wall of dark windows, most likely looking out onto the city. Mani could see the twinkling lights laid out in the pattern leading to the center circle.

There was a soft sound over in the shadows, and Mani turned to see a small figure step out of the shadows and walk slowly towards her. The person was the same size as her, and as they approached her, she could see suddenly that it was a boy who looked to be her age. He looked incredibly familiar. Mani saw that he had the same colored hair as her, and the same eyes! He was smiling, and she noticed that they shared almost the same smile. He looked like a picture of her father, when he was Mani's age, she had once seen.

Mani put her hand over her pocket that carried Em, and Em rustled around, pressing into her hand to comfort her. As Mani watched, the boy pressed his hand over the pocket of his own sweater. Slowly, Mani cupped Em and drew her carefully out of her pocket, holding her in front of herself. As she watched the boy get closer and closer, she saw that he too had pulled something out of his pocket and was holding it in his hands.

Mani and the boy came face to face, his face a big smile and hers a big question. He opened his hands, and there in his cupped palms was a snit! It was as white as a sweet dinner roll, with a pink nose and a black stripe all the way down its back. Mani copied his movements and opened her hands to show off Em in all her dark loveliness. As they both watched, the snits sniffed each other and seemed to like what they saw, choosing after a minute to scramble up onto their child's shoulder to watch and wait.

"Hi Mani," the boy said, still smiling. "I've heard a lot about you! I'm glad you're here safe. I was worried, and so was Bo."

"Mani, meet my son Rani," said Uncle Jock.

Chapter 9
A New Friend

Mani was shocked to meet yet another new family member. Rani stuck out his had to shake hers, and as they shook Mani felt an electric tingle pass through their hands. Now she smiled too, mirroring the enormous grin on her cousin's face.

"Rani, can you show Mani to her room? I have some important phone calls to make. I will see you both in the morning," said Uncle Jock. Rani turned and gave his father a tight hug, and got a kiss on the head in return.

"Come on, Mani," said Rani in an excited voice, "I'll show you your room, it's right next to mine. Do you want to take the elevator again? I bet you're super tired. Wait 'til you see your room! We've been getting it ready for a whole month! I'm so excited to finally get to hang out with someone my own age. It can get so boring here."

Mani could hardly keep up with her cousin as he herded her into the elevator, pressed buttons, and chattered away. He told her about his book collection, his crystal collection, his machines, and something called 'sweets.'

"Dad said that I can take you into the town tomorrow and show you around. He even gave me money for the bakery and some other stuff for you!" The elevator opened onto a new floor and Rani took off down the hallway, Mani trying to keep up.

"Here's my room," he gestured. Mani could see through the open door that the room was a mess of things: machines, rocks, books, toys, and many items she couldn't name. "And here is yours. Right next to mine. There's even a connecting door!" Enthusiastically, he dragged her into a room that was lit with a single lamp by the bed. As Mani watched, Rani walked over to the wall that separated her room from his. He pushed aside a massive hanging curtain to reveal a small door, a door he opened to show her that his room was indeed on the other side.

"If you ever need anything, you can just pop through. Isn't it great? And there are all of these secret passages all over the castle I can show you! You can go almost anywhere without being seen. I sneak into the kitchen for snacks all the time and they never catch me-" Rani seemed to realize that Mani was suddenly overwhelmed and exhausted. His voice trailed off and he started inching towards the door.

"Check out your bathroom, it's over there. How about I come get you for breakfast?" Mani nodded. Rani left quietly then, leaving her in the silence and the near dark.

Once again, tired and alone, Mani crawled onto the bed and curled up into a ball. With Em snuggled into her neck she finally fell asleep, hoping that the new day would bring answers to the questions that she had about her parents and how she would be getting them back.

★ ★ ★

Even though she was bone tired, Mani awoke early and managed to have a bath and wash up. Even Em had a soak in the sink, circling under the water and blowing bubbles. Her cute little bathroom had everything she needed, even a toothbrush and hair ties to put her hair back into a ponytail.

Back in the main room, she discovered that there were fresh clothes in the dresser and shoes in the closet. She chose new jeans and a soft shirt, as well as a new sweater with pockets, since the one she was wearing was starting to smell. Socks and sneakers with funny ties finished her outfit. Now that she was clean and in new clothes, Mani felt confident that she could get on with the next part of her adventure: discovering the castle and getting answers about her parents. Oh, and eating too!

There was a loud knock on her door and Mani opened it to reveal a tired-looking Rani. His hair was sticking up on one side and his snit was sitting on his shoulder, watching her. Rani immediately started talking, asking her questions about her sleep and her life under the dome and anything else he could think of. By the time they reached the floor with the breakfast room Mani was definitely hungry, and Rani was looking more awake.

At the table, Uncle Jock was working on some papers and drinking coffee. Mani and Rani helped themselves to some breakfast on the side table and joined him. Uncle Jock's eyebrows went up as he counted the six pieces of bacon on Mani's plate. She blushed.

"Mrs. Crank never made bacon at the mansion," she explained.

Uncle Jock laughed. "She never does. Perhaps I should have known that someone who doesn't like bacon cannot be trusted!" He winked at Mani and she smiled back, munching her beloved bacon.

After breakfast, with money in their pockets for exploring and a stern warning from Uncle Jock not to eat too many sweets before lunch, the cousins headed out into the city.

"What are these sweets you keep talking about?" asked Mani.

Rani's eyes bugged out of his head. "You don't know what candy is?" he asked.

"Oh, candy." Said Mani. "You mean like honey?"

"No, I mean like sweet things in different shapes and flavours! Like gumdrops and gobstoppers and licorice!"

Mani looked confused. "There were no foods like that under the dome. Only fruits and vegetables, fish, and honey from the bee hives. Sometimes we had cake or cookies."

Rani got really excited then. He asked Mani which shop she would like to go to first then, the candy shop or the other shops that they had been talking about the night before.

"Definitely the candy shop!" declared Mani.

Grinning Rani led her to a brightly colored store where the owner seemed to know Rani very well. When he asked for an assortment, she packaged up several paper bags that held a variety of the delights Mani had been hearing about.

Then they were out into the city, visiting the bookshop, the rock and gem shop, a bakery, and a gadget place. As they went, they sampled the candies, eating more and more as the morning progressed. When the clock struck 11, Rani steered Mani back to the castle in the wall, saying that they needed to be back for lunch.

The only candy left now were the gumballs, which Rani had said to save until the end as they lasted a long time. Both cousins were feeling ill by then, the masses of sugar in their bellies making alarming grumbles.

"Oh, I feel awful. I don't think I can eat lunch," said Rani, "I'm going to be in big trouble with my dad."

"Ugh," moaned Mani, "Let's just try to eat lunch. Maybe he won't find out."

Uncle Jock watched them both like a hawk at lunch, making sure they ate their sandwiches and fruit. Miserably, Mani and Rani choked down the huge cookies that were for dessert. Then they excused themselves and rode the elevator up to their floor, where they went into Rani's room and lay on the floor in agony.

Rani finally crawled into his bathroom and retched up his lunch, all of the candy, and the giant cookie. Bo had deserted him by then and was sleeping on the pillow on his bed, Em curled up next to him. Unable to hold out any longer, Mani ran to the bathroom and threw up everything she had eaten, down to the last speck of gumdrop.

"I'm never going to eat candy again!" declared Rani. "Or at least not until tomorrow."

Mani laughed weakly, and they both crawled out of the bathroom to lay on the bed, close to the sleeping snits.

Soon they were asleep as well, the late night and the morning's escapade taking its toll.

Chapter 10

A Plan

Late in the afternoon, Mani awoke to find both snits on the pillow gone and Rani still passed out. She lay on the bed thinking for a long time. Then she shook him awake gently, letting him come fully awake before she asked him a serious question.

"Can you find a way to listen in on your dad if he is making plans about my parents? I am worried, and I want to know what is going to happen. I've only had my parents all these years, what if I never see them again?" Mani started to cry softly, missing Em at that moment.

Rani took her hand and squeezed it tightly. Mani felt better right away just talking to him. Now she suddenly realized she had a friend to talk to, not just a snit, and she had family that could possibly help. Rani was smart and he would know all sorts of things that might be done.

"I know a passage to a vent on the wall in my Dad's office. Let's go listen and see what we can find out." He led the way to the secret doorway between the rooms, and opened it, showing Mani that you could turn into the wall space on the inside of the doors to find a new passage. "I hope you're good with stairs and small spaces. These go on for miles! You can even find a way down out the back of the other side of the castle to the ocean. We keep boats in a boathouse with a dock, but I have secret way to get there. "

"I'm fine with small spaces," said Mani, "I lived under a bowl under the sea, remember? There was no extra space anywhere. Our bathroom was smaller than the ones here and we shared it. I'm not too good in the dark though."

Rani went back into his room and dug around in one of his dressers. He came back with two lamps, similar to the ones that were used under the domes. After he handed one to Mani, he shook his vigorously and it started to glow a soft pink. Mani shook hers as well and it too glowed, but a soft blue.

"It's special crystal that is luminescent when you agitate it," Rani explained. "You'll have to shake it once in a while, but it will never run out. And if you open the lamp and pick a crystal to drop into water, it will glow forever. Its part of my collection, and I invented the lamp so I could explore the passages here without needing batteries."

Mani was impressed. "What other gadgets do you have?" she asked.

Rani just laughed. "Tons. I'll show you later."

With that, he closed the door behind them and started leading Mani through the passageway. And he wasn't kidding, they went on for ages. They went down three flights of rickety stairs and down and around countless loops of passages until he stopped. There was a vent into a room, set low on the wall, and the light was coming into the passage from the room.

"This is Dad's office," whispered Rani, crouching down and pointing through the vent.

They pressed up close to the vent and looked through the slats. Sure enough, there was a big wooden desk covered in papers, and Uncle Jock in a leather chair behind it. He was speaking into a phone, leaning over his desk and looking very serious.

"What is the plan, Major?" he was asking. He listened intently for what felt like an eternity, then spoke again. "So we know that they are being held in the mansion dungeon holding cells. Do the Striker group want anything in return for their release?" Again, Uncle Jock listened to whoever was on the other end of the phone. Then he nodded. "And you want to wait another two days? Why?" Finally, he hung up the phone and rubbed his forehead. He was quiet as he leaned back in his chair and stared at the ceiling.

In the passageway, Rani motioned to Mani to follow him. Then he silently led her back the way they came, reaching the familiarity of Rani's bedroom as quickly as possible. Once there, he looked at Mani silently, waiting for once to let her speak before he started talking.

Mani started pacing in the room. Her mind was moving in all directions, thinking about who and what and where and how. Finally, she stopped.

"Do you know how to get back to the mansion?" she asked Rani, her face scrunched up in thought.

"Yeeessss…" said Rani slowly. "You can go up the coast by boat, on the road in a vehicle, or in an airship. It can take three hours or more."

"Can you work any of those machines?" Mani asked hopefully.

"Only the boat," said Rani, "and only my little one. I could try to drive my dad's fast one, but we'd have to steal the keys and get past the soldiers down there."

Both cousins were quiet for a moment. Bo and Em appeared from wherever they had been, choosing to scramble up into their separate pocket hideouts and hunker down for a nap.

In the end, it was Mani who spoke. "I don't know what to do, Rani. I need to do something to rescue my parents. But I feel like it would be such a hard thing to do. Will you help me make a plan? I don't even know what I would need…" she trailed off.

Rani looked earnestly at Mani and said "We need to see a plan for the mansion, the blueprints. Then we can see the best way to get there if we use a boat. And we need to make a list of things to take along to help us out. Let's wait until my dad leaves the office and check out the plans for the mansion. Sound good?" Mani nodded.

So, back into the passageway they went, down to the vent in the wall outside the office. As they peered inside, they realized Uncle Jock was already gone, his chair empty behind the desk but the papers still spread out over it.

Fishing in his other pocket and juggling his light, Rani took out a tool and started prying the vent off the wall. It popped off and landed on the floor, and the cousins wriggled through the opening into the room, falling as well onto the soft carpet.

Moving quickly, Rani ran to the desk and looked through the papers. In an instant he had selected a large sheet, rolled it up, and tucked it into his shirt. Then he rearranged the papers on the desk so it looked like nothing had been taken.

The last thing they did was to pop the vent back onto the wall, making sure there were no marks or dust or dirt smears on the wall or carpet. Then they tiptoed over to the door, cracked it open to see if anyone was in the hallway, and eased out, shutting the door with a soft click.

Both of the cousins were walking down the hallway when they heard "Where are you two going?" from behind them.

They froze, staring in guilt at each other. As they turned around, they realized Uncle Jock had quietly caught up to them. He looked at both of their faces sternly.

"I know what you've been doing," he said.

Mani's heart was beating like thunder in her ears. Rani had gone sheet-white and was opening and closing his mouth silently, trying to say something.

"Both of you ate too much candy this morning, didn't you? The housekeeper said that your bathroom was quite a mess this afternoon when she went in to tidy up!" Uncle Jock continued.

Mani and Rani looked at each other in relief. They looked guilty when as faced Uncle Jock, and both nodded at him silently.

"Well, I hope you've learned your lesson, both of you. I'm going to be very busy over the next few days, so you two are going to have to be good and look after yourselves as I try to figure out how to get the king and queen back. Can you do that?"

When the children nodded at him, he motioned them to follow him back down the hall, reminding them that it was dinnertime already. They went slowly, Rani trying to make sure the large roll of paper under his shirt didn't show or make any noise.

Their plan was safe, for now.

Chapter 11

A Special Package

Supper was a quiet torture for both of the cousins. Uncle Jock looking gloomy, his brows drawn together over his angry eyes. He was reading another piece of mail as he ate, and off to the side was a large package that had been opened, its papers spread across one corner of the massive table as Uncle Jock pretended to eat but actually worked. Everyone ate in silence, and there was minimal noise except the ticking of the grandfather clock in the corner and the scraping of fork on fine plates.

Finally, Rani asked to be excused. His father nodded absently, still silent. When Mani looked at him and opened her mouth to ask he just nodded at her as well, and she rose from the table quickly to make her getaway.

As they exited the dining room, both children broke into a run for the stairs. Neither wanted to wait for the elevator, and Rani was already talking a mile a minute to Mani as they huffed and puffed up the flights of stairs to the safety of their room.

"Did you see that large parcel at the dining table? It came from the coastal town where the mansion is, it came from Dral! I had a great idea when we were eating. Let's get to my room and we can work it out together," said Rani excitedly.

Once they were in his room, Rani went over to his work table covered in gadgets and started to comb through the piles of parts and tools.

"What are you looking for?" asked Mani, as she joined him to look at the items. She had no idea what most of them were, but if helping him meant helping the plan, she would do it.

"I need the smoke bombs I made for Founders Day! I know they are here. Here they are!" He held up two round metal objects each as large as his fist and waved them at her. "I put ones like these together to make a large puff of colored smoke during our day of celebration. They pop open and make an awesome sound and a big cloud of color, but won't hurt anyone. With a little tinkering, I could get them on a trigger so they will pop open…add a little bit of liquid colored dye…" Rani trailed off as he turned to a set of cabinets behind the worktable and started pulling out packets and jars of ink. "This stuff is the best! It takes forever to wear off and the person who gets hit gets so mad. It'll be great!"

"Slow down!" said Mani, "What are you planning to do? I though we were going to use your dad's boat to get to the mansion?"

"Oh no, this will be even better," exclaimed Rani. "I have a friend at school whose father works at the post office. When we were eating, I was thinking about the mail, and I suddenly thought that if we could just send a package with some color bombs on a trigger to the Mansion, we could tag along in the night delivery truck with it. We would get delivered right to where we want to go, and the package could be a distraction…" Once again Rani trailed off as he began wiring the round balls together and placing a triggering unit on them.

The Girl From the Bottom of the Sea

"I remember Mrs. Crank. She's the only one who goes out to pick up the mail in the mornings, at precisely 8 am when it's delivered. If we address it to her, she will be the one who opens it. She runs that house, and if she gets mad everyone gets in trouble. If there are soldiers there guarding your parents, all we have to do is make Mrs. Crank mad, and then she'll scream for them, they'll come running. Then we can sneak in and find the way to the cells under the mansion. Where's my other kit?" Rani was digging through another drawer again. "We have to hurry if we want to make the evening delivery time!"

"Tell me what I can pack up or do," said Mani. She was desperate to help now.

Rani showed her his backpack and directed her to fill it with his small medical kit (they might need it, he said), the two light orbs ("In case the lights go out."), the bag of gumballs that were left over, snacks for the snits, and some other items.

After the bombs were wrapped and placed into a box, Rani taped it shut with the trigger wire under the tape. As soon as Mrs. Crank open the box, the wire would pull out, and BOOM! Mani didn't even ask what color Rani had used in them; anything that would scare that mean old lady was splendid. Then he addressed the package to the mansion and told Mani to change into all black clothes.

"Remember, an outfit with pockets since we're bringing Bo and Em with us." he said. "We might need them if we get stuck." He had started changing as Mani hurried through the adjoining door to her room, and Mani changed herself in record time. When she returned to her cousin's room she found him changed, with backpack on, and rummaging through the drawer in his desk this time.

"Aha!" He held up a golden key, then slid it into the pocket where Bo was curled up. "Let's go!" Mani grabbed the parcel as they left.

The Girl From the Bottom of the Sea

It was back into the hallway and down the stairs as quietly as they could. Every flight of stairs, Rani would stop and listen for any sign of his father or staff. In the end, they met no one and saw no sign of any staff as they let themselves out of the castle and hurried off into the city as the sun was setting.

'Hurry hurry hurry hurry,' the voice was shouting inside Mani's head by the time they reached the post office. The light was still on inside, and the 'open' sign was still displayed in the window. Rani pushed the door open and they slipped inside.

Behind the counter, the kind old lady greeted Rani by name and smiled at Mani. When Rani showed her the package and the address, she frowned and told them that the delivery truck was getting ready to leave right then if they wanted it to go that night.

"Could you make sure it does?" Rani asked in his most hopeful voice, giving her a big charming smile.

When she left through the back door with the parcel, Rani motioned silently for Mani to follow him through the same door. They crept after the postmistress, listening around the corner as she spoke with the driver of the delivery van. After he accepted the package, and the postmistress had walked back through to the front, Rani and Mani crept around the corner, checked to see the driver wasn't around, and popped open the back door of the van. They climbed in, closing the doors behind them and picking their way through the piles of parcels and bags of mail. There, in an open spot behind a rather large box, they settled, quiet as church mice and holding their breath. In their pockets, both Bo and Em were as still as stones.

Rani reached out and took Mani's hand in his. They looked at each other as the driver hopped into his seat, rocking the van from side to side for a few moments. Finally, the engine started and the vehicle began to roll away.

"Cross your fingers!" Rani whispered, and Mani was sure that both of them did, all the way to Dral.

Chapter 12

The Mansion

It felt like the longest night of Mani's life in the back of that van. Even with Rani there holding her hand in the dark, it was hard to tell how much time was passing. Around them, the smell of paper and cotton mail sacks was strong and somewhat comforting. It reminded Mani of school under the dome. After a while Rani pulled over a lumpy mail bag and they leaned onto it, trying to fall asleep. He soon did with no problem, but Mani could not. Her mind was moving and moving, thinking about her parents, her life under the dome, the escape they had made together, and the one that she had made with Uncle Jock. In just one month, her drab and boring life had been transformed in to one of adventure, amazement, new family and friends. She let her thoughts reach out, forward, towards her parents and where they were now, and what she would do to get them back. She decided that she would do almost anything, even trip that evil Mrs. Crank, or lock her in a closet, or, or, or… Finally Mani's thoughts came back to her and she found some peace, falling asleep on the mail sack.

It was the grinding and bumping that woke the children. It must have been early morning, because there was a lightening of the sky outside of the van's back windows. They could feel the van slowing, and rather o. R than moving straight, it began making turns, first some rights and then a left. Finally, it ground to a halt with a soft screech.

Rani and Mani became instantly alert, waiting for the back doors to open. After five or six minutes, when nothing happened, Rani crept to the van doors and peered out the window. No one was there. Both children jumped out of the van and took off down the alley that it was parked in before they could be found or seen. And once they were on the street they slowed to a regular walk and pretended to be out early on an errand in the early morning.

"I'm starving!" said Mani.

"Me too. Let's go to a bakery and grab something before we have to trek up the hill. We'll have to be careful that we aren't seen or recognized though. Lots of people know my face, and I'm sure that as a princess your picture has been published by now."

With that, he pulled out two caps from his backpack, and they put them on, Mani tucking her hair into it and Rani pulling it low over his forehead. He steered them to a small bakery so busy with the early morning crowd that no one bothered to stop and look at two kids buying breakfast rolls and sweet buns that they stuck into their pockets. They quickly washed up in the bathrooms there and then headed out onto the sidewalk again, prepared for the steep walk up the hill to the mansion. As they started walking, the clock in the town square chimed seven bells. They had one hour until their special package would be delivered, and they needed to reach the mansion before it arrived.

Mani remembered the hill that the mansion was on, and Rani obviously knew how to get to it from the town. He pointed out a huge public garden that stretched up the side of the hill, and then they began trudging up it. After they reached the top of the garden, Rani turned them onto a side street that wound around the wall that circled the mansion.

"We will have to find a way over the wall," he said, a frown on his face. "And fast! The package should be delivered soon."

"Here!" Mani pointed out an overgrown part of the wall that had a tree growing close to it. "We can climb over and drop into the back garden."

They scrambled up the tree and over in seconds, then dropped to the ground in the dense garden bushes. Keeping low, they crept along until the back entrance to the kitchen part of the mansion was in sight. There, a single soldier with a rifle was walking along the back of the house, looking seriously grumpy.

"Looks like he didn't get any bacon this morning either," Mani said. She couldn't help herself and started to giggle quietly. "Mrs. Crank is such a terrible cook!"

Rani shushed her. "There he goes, let's make a dash for it!" With that they took off for the door, crossing the lawn with the speed of jackrabbits. Rani took a tube out of his backpack and bent the end over, then used it to look into the window from around the corner.

"No one there, they must be setting out breakfast!" he said in a hushed voice. Mani let them in the door and they snuck through the kitchen. Rani grabbed a handful of warm cookies as they went past the counter, shoving them into his pocket.

"Let's see if Mrs. Crank notices that!" he said as they tiptoed down the hallway to the back stairs.

Once in the back stairwell, Rani whipped out the blueprint of the mansion and took a look at the marks that he had made.

"If we go down these stairs all the way, we'll reach the door that leads to the front part of the underground holding cells. There's a supply closet we can hide in there and see what is going on. Hopefully there won't be a soldier sitting there." They were both panting as they continued down the four flights of stairs, not stopping until they reached the door Rani was talking about.

Once again, he pulled out his bent spyglass and used it to peer through the small window in the door. Then he looked at Mani sadly.

"There are three soldiers. I wasn't expecting three." He sounded gloomy.

Mani's heart dropped. They had come all this way and now they had to stop?

Somewhere in another part of the house there was a loud boom, followed by some screaming.

"The bomb!" the cousins said excitedly. Rani looked through the window.

"Get behind the door!" he said as he shoved Mani into the corner. In a second the staircase door banged open, hiding the two children momentarily as the three soldiers charged up the stair case, rifles at the ready. Their radios were squawking loudly, Mrs. Crank shouting at them to hurry up. As soon as the soldiers were gone, the cousins darted around the door and thundered over to the locked doorway the soldiers had been watching.

"This leads to the holding cells," Rani exclaimed as he fished around in his pocket for a moment. Out came the golden key from his desk drawer. He pushed it into the lock on the door, pressed a button on the head and said "One, two, three," then turned the key. There was a heavy click and the lock opened, much to Mani's amazement.

"It's my master key," Rani held up the key that he had now removed. "I plug it in, press the button, and it makes a new key inside. I got it at a gadget shop, but I'd never had a chance to use it. Awesome!"

Mani and he flew through the open door, shutting and locking it behind them so that no one would know that they had been there.

Then they began walking down the hallway, looking into the windows on the doors that lined each side. Finally, at the very end door, Mani cried out, "Mama! Papa!"

Mani's mother crowded up to the window in the door, staring at Mani and Rani with a stunned face. Rani ignored her and used his golden key to unlock the door and open it as quickly as possible.

Once inside, the children realized why Mani's father had not come to the window. He was sitting on the narrow bed in the cell holding his arm, blood dripping onto the floor from his hand.

"Don't let the door close!" he yelled at the children. Rani stopped short and caught the door seconds before it closed behind them.

"We have to keep the door from closing," the king said weakly. "Do you have anything that could plug the deadbolt hole?" His face was pale and he looked as if he was ready to faint, not escape.

Rani held the door from closing, then handed Mani his backpack. As she took it, she realized that Em was clambering out of her pocket, and Bo was climbing out of Rani's. Both of the snits took off out the crack in the door, heading towards where the soldiers would be when they came back.

"Get out the bag of gumballs," Rani instructed Mani.

When she fished them out, he pulled out a handful and started cramming them into the deadbolt hole on the doorframe. Once it was full he carefully let the door close, then pulled it open to test that it kept the door from locking. It worked!

Now Mani approached her parents, her mother opening her arms for a hug, and her father reaching out with his good hand to stroke her hair.

"We are so glad to see you!" her mother said. "When we awoke in the cell without you, there was no way to find out where you were. Mrs. Crank must have drugged our dessert, but we knew that you didn't eat it, nor did Uncle Jock, so we hoped and prayed that you had escaped! How did you get here?"

"No time for that!" Rani was fishing in his backpack again.

This time, Mani's parents looked at Rani and really saw him. Their faces registered surprise as they saw how much he looked like Mani, how he was the same height with the same hair color and smile. It was Mani's turn to deliver a surprise to someone as she told them that Rani was her cousin, Uncle Jock's son. Both of her parents were flabbergasted.

"Well, I would have known you were related to us just from your looks," Mani's mother said. "We will have to have a chat with your father about this secret when we meet him. If we ever do…" she trailed off, looking grim.

Rani had finally extracted the medical kit from his backpack, and run over to the king. He knelt down in front of him and opened up the kit, pulling out a metal can.

"Hold out your hand, I want to see the injury," he asked.

As the king held out his hand, Mani could see that the skin was torn all across his hand, the flesh ragged and still seeping blood.

"I tried to stop the door from closing the last time we were returned to the cell, a couple of hours ago. They had taken me to ask me questions and get me to open the royal safe so that they could take the money and the jewels, but I wouldn't give in, so they dragged me back to the cells. Unfortunately, the door closed on my hand. I think the bones are broken inside, and it won't stop bleeding."

Rani took the metal can and pressed the top. There was a soft hissing, and liquid flowed out of a small hole. As it flowed onto the king's hand, it began to cover the wound with a thick, shiny substance. As everyone watched, the wound began to pull back together, healing up until there was no sign of any injury. The king flexed his hand, checking it and finding that it was perfectly healed. Mani and her parents were stunned as Rani then fished out a container and shook out two orange pills.

"Take these," he ordered. "They will help with any pain and help your body have energy. You're going to need it; we need to get going!"

As he spoke, Em and Bo came scurrying into the room, squeaking like crazy. They ran to the corner behind where the door opened and stopped there, squeaking and looking at Mani and Rani.

In a flash, the children snatched up their stuff and raced to the snits. They scooped them up and stood silently in the corner, waiting to see what the snits were warning them about. Sure enough, a soldier came to the window in the door of the cell and glared inside, looking at the king and queen sitting on the narrow bed in the corner. The king was pretending to be injured, hunching over his hand. But the soldier did not see the cousins hiding around the corner, holding their snits and their breath as they waited for him to leave. Ten seconds, eleven, twelve. Mani was sweating and counting, terrified of being discovered, or of the door being found to be unlocked.

Finally, the soldier turned and walked away, his boots clomping down the hallway as he returned to his post.

Everyone let out the breath that they were holding.

"Now what?" asked Mani.

"Now we make our escape!" said Rani.

Chapter Thirteen

Fight or Flight

Everyone in the cell looked at each other for a moment, thinking about escape.

"How can we escape if we know that there are three guards at the end of the hall? And where would we go?" asked the queen. "If we try to go upstairs we're sure to meet more soldiers and just get thrown back in here."

"The plans of the mansion show that there is another underground storage garage one level up from here." Said the king as he and Rani sat looking at the blueprints spread out on the floor. "If we could find a way to send the guards off, we could make a dash for it. There is another passage out of the garage, down the back way, all the way to the beach below the cliff that the mansion backs onto."

"And we only have a little bit of time until they bring our breakfast," the queen said with worry in her voice. "We need to get moving before the soldiers actually come in here to feed us and find that we have more guests then they were planning to feed!"

"I have an idea," said Mani hesitantly. She had been thinking about how all the other cells she had seen were empty. "We could sneak over into another cell and wait. They won't think that we can get out, and that we would go into another cell. And they might go away to find you if they think that you have escaped."

Rani and the king nodded as they thought about the idea, and the queen drew Mani back into her arms to embrace her again.

"Pack up all the gear Rani, let's get ready to move," the king said, looking at his watch. "We have twenty minutes until they come in with breakfast."

Packed up and moving towards the door, they stayed as quiet as they could. At the door, the king motioned to Rani to get out his key, and he slowly pulled the door open and looked carefully down the hall towards the entryway door and the guards. Then he closed the door again.

"You go first Rani, use your key and open the door across from us. Then jam the frame with the gum again and wait for us. Mani can go next, then the queen, then me. Everyone ready?" They all looked at each other and nodded.

Quietly, the king opened the door again, checked to make sure no guard was looking through the window, then motioned to Rani. Quick as lightening Rani was through the door, across the hall, and opening the empty cell. As Mani held her breath, he jammed more gumballs into the door lock hole, then motioned for her. Again, the king watched the window down the hall, then gave Mani the okay. She scooted across silently, standing behind Rani and the half-open doorway.

Back across the hall, the queen was getting ready to cross when the king pulled her back inside and shut the door suddenly. Startled, Rani shoved Mani farther into the cell and shut their door as well. They flattened themselves against the wall by the door and waited with baited breath as they heard the heavy clomp of a soldier's boots come down the hallway and stop in front of the cell the king and queen were in.

For a few moments, there was nothing, and then the sound of heavy footsteps moved back down the hallway to the entryway.

In seconds, both the king and queen pushed through the empty cell door, rushing as soundlessly as possible.

"That was close," the king huffed, "The guard came to check us one more time before breakfast. I thought we would be caught!"

Now it was time to wait, and that was hard. All four of them sat up against the wall that the cell door was on, listening and huddling together. It seemed like an eternity, sitting in the quietness of the empty cell, everyone breathing as quietly as they could as they wondered if the plan would work. Then Mani heard the return of the soldier with the heavy tread, now bearing breakfast on a clattering tray. He stomped down the hall and they heard him stop at the cell door where he was expecting to find the king and queen cowering. Instead, he found an empty cell, gumballs jammed into the frame.

With a shout, he threw the tray of food onto the floor of the room and ran down the hallway, alerting his compatriots to the missing royals. When the shouting and stomping feet faded away into silence, the king looked at them all and said, "Well, it's now or never. Let's go!"

And with that, they were out the door, down the hall, through the entryway, and into the stairwell. They barely paused to make sure that there was no one in the stairwell or coming down as they pounded up the one flight of stairs. On that landing, Rani fished out his golden key and used it to open another door marked Garage Level 1. Then they burst through as a group into what looked to Mani like another massive storage room full of vehicles, machines, and crates of who-knows-what.

"Let's grab an inflatable boat and some paddles and load up one of the carts," the king directed. He pointed at a large rubber bundle and some paddles while he himself headed over to a four-seated cart. The queen and Mani grabbed four paddles as Rani dragged the rubber package over to the cart, and the king threw them all into the back. Then, everyone jumped into the cart and the king started it up, driving to the far end of the garage towards a dark opening barely large enough to let their vehicle through.

"Hang on!" shouted the king as he popped the headlights on and they barrelled through. "If I remember right, it'll be about ten minutes to the beach."

Behind them, the door into the garage from the stairs burst open and soldiers flooded into the garage, shouting at them and each other as they saw the royals making their getaway.

"They're after us!" screamed Mani. She grabbed Rani and they held tight to each other as the king floored the gas pedal and zoomed through the darkened passage. The headlights of the cart were bouncing wildly off the walls, reflecting off the rough black surface in wild shadows and shapes.

It was a shorter ride than anticipated and as soon as they saw the light at the end of the tunnel, they all leaned forward in the speeding cart, willing it to go faster. Rocketing through the opening onto the grey pebbled beach, they hurtled close to the waves pounding the shore. The cart lurched to a sudden stop and everyone piled out, grabbing the raft and paddles. It took both children to drag the raft to the water. The king threw the strap off the rubber package and pulled a ripcord on the side. Within five seconds the black raft had inflated fully, and the children clambered in it as it floated on the edge of the water, the queen and king pushing it further and then hopping in themselves. Everyone started paddling like mad.

Bang! Bang! Crack! Gunshots sounded in the air.

The soldiers were on the beach now as well, jumping out of other carts and pointing rifles at the group in the raft as they tried to escape. There were a dozen of them and they were all armed.

"Hold your fire!" one soldier shouted. "We need them alive!"

Bang!

One more shot was fired and with horror, Mani and her group saw that the raft now had a large hole in the side and was deflating rapidly. They were devastated. The paddling stopped. There was no escape now for them. Reluctantly, they began to paddle slowly back to shore as the boat started taking water on and finally sank. Wet, tired, silent, all four waded out of the surf holding their paddles loosely in their hands.

The soldiers were on them instantly, grabbing them roughly and tying their hand behind their backs. Mani was shivering and Rani's head was drooping. Her father was holding his head up though, glaring at the men holding rifles and dragging the queen away to a cart.

BWAAAHHH! A loud bullhorn sounded from out on the water.

Every person on the beach turned to see the sea suddenly filled with speeding black military rafts aiming for the shore. They were packed with militia wearing the royal uniform of black, red, and gold, and every one of them was holding a gun. There must have been at least a hundred of them, Mani thought. She felt the hands holding her suddenly release, and she turned to find that all of the soldiers had dropped their guns and were holding their hands up in surrender.

As the group of boats from the sea beached themselves, a figure leaped from the prow of one and stormed up the beach. It was Uncle Jock! Followed by the armed guards, he reached Rani with great speed and swept him up into a hug.

The rebel soldiers were swiftly overcome and relieved of their weapons. They lined up silently, grim looks on their faces, watched by the Royal Army. At the same time, Uncle Jock cut the ropes binding the wet group of Royals and released them.

"How did you know to come?" the king asked his brother.

"Well, once I realized that my son and niece were gone and had taken one of my most important blueprints," he stared at Rani and Mani seriously, "I knew that there was no more time. We were already planning a rescue from the beach and up the passage to the cells, by force, but we had no idea that you would be here already. And we weren't planning to attack until tomorrow, but with the children already gone and probably captured for all we knew, we had to push up the schedule."

"I've never been happier to see you!" The king shook his brother's hand and then turned to his wife and daughter. "I've had enough of being a prisoner and being wet. Let's go back to the mansion and get comfortable."

With that, the army loaded up the carts with as many of them as possible, and the royals, and left the rest to guard the rebels.

Speaking into his radio, Uncle Jock confirmed that the other part of the Royal Army had successfully surrounded and then captured the mansion from the front of the house, finding most of the rebel soldiers eating breakfast and one very angry Mrs. Crank who was – hilariously, Mani thought, - covered in blue, purple, and green dye. The mansion holding cells were now full of rebels and a cranky Mrs. Crank, who kept shouting about "those awful children!" After Rani had a whispered conversation with his father to tell him about the gumballs in the cell doors, Uncle Jock laughed and instructed the soldiers under his command to not only clean them out but to always check each door.

After all of that, it was just a matter of returning to the mansion for clean dry clothes and a decent meal. The king was busy with his brother taking care of military matters, and the queen was resting in her room. Rani and Mani were camped out in her room on the second floor, eating sweets that Rani had found in his room and talking about their adventure. Their snits were sleeping curled up together on the pillow, most likely, Mani thought, worn out from all the running and chasing.

"I think I've had enough adventure for a little while!" said Mani, helping herself to another chocolate. The ones filled with marshmallow were her favorites, and she had eaten three in a row. Abruptly, she pushed away the candy bag. "Maybe I should stop eating these or I might have one in the bathroom, throwing up again!"

Rani laughed but folded up the top of the candy bag and stowed it in a drawer.

"Now you just have to learn all about how to be a royal, huh?" he poked Mani. "And wear jewels with everything!" He pretended to put on a crown and wave at people. She giggled.

"And you'll have to teach me all about your gadgets!" she said, poking him back. "I want to build stuff and learn everything about The Over. Maybe even about The Under as well. I did live there. I don't know why The Under and The Over can't be friends. I'd like to go back and see my friends one day."

"Anything is possible!" said Rani.

And Mani nodded, thinking that the whole world was stretching out before her like an endless puzzle, just waiting to be discovered - by her, and by those that she loved as well.

Epilogue

It had been a month since the grand rescue at the mansion. The royals had moved to their main castle, the one built into the wall of the volcano ring. Mani's parents were busy with meetings and appearances and government sittings. Mani and Rani had settled into regular schooling with the tutors that came in to teach. But one day, something was wrong.

"Have you seen Em?" Mani asked Rani as she came running into his room. "I haven't seen her for a whole day, and that is unusual. She's been sleeping a lot lately, and every time she sits in my pocket, she feels like she weighs twice as much! Have you seen Bo?"

Rani shook his head. "I was coming to find you! I can't find him either. Something is wrong."

Mani looked so worried, her face scrunched up in fear. Both her and Rani were attached to their snits in a deep way. They rarely ever went anywhere without them, and they had come to rely on the snits to watch out for them as well. She was racking her brain, trying to think of where Em might go. She always left her sink full of water in her bathroom, so that Em could go for a swim any time she wanted.

"Let's check my bathroom," Mani finally decided. "If we find one we might find the other." Both children hurried to the little ensuite in Mani's room and started looking around. The sink was full of water, but no snits. The tub was empty, as was the linen closet.

"Stop! Listen!" Mani commanded.

There was soft squeaking under the sink, in the cabinet. Mani opened the doors and there, in a nest made of towels, were Em and Bo. And with them were two brand new little snit babies!

"Oh, my goodness! No wonder you were getting heavy!" Mani said. Em watched Mani as she reached in to touch the babies. Both were so tiny and had shiny skin. One was white with black spots and the other was black with white spots.

"Well, a family!" Rani said, apparently bursting with happiness. "We have two more mouths to start sneaking sweet rolls for now!"

Mani sat on the floor, the joy shining out of her face. When Rani noticed the look on her face, he asked her what she was thinking.

"I was thinking that today has been an amazing day!" Mani looked at her cousin with a big smile. "Can you keep a secret?"

When Rani nodded, she continued: "My mother told me today that she is expecting a baby too. I'm going to be a big sister! My brother or sister will be here sometime in winter, and I'm so excited. More family for me."

"Wow!" Rani was amazed, "Another cousin for me! And here you thought that you wouldn't be having any adventures soon."

The cousins laughed, and Mani thought her heart would burst with happiness. More snits, another baby on the way: these things meant more love today and more to come. And Mani liked that very much, very much indeed.

THE END

Did you enjoy this story? I sure enjoyed telling it as a story cycle to the kids in Mrs. Striemer's Grade 1 and 2 class! You see, years ago, when I camped with my own children, I would tell a story cycle filled with wonder and adventure as we sat around the fire under the stars. They were purely oral stories, made up on the fly and told with so much emotion, and my children loved every one. This story is the last series that I started before we stopped camping regularly and my children grew older. I never had a chance to finish it. Fast forward to an opportunity to keep a class enthralled for ten minutes at the end of the day - and a desire to put the story on paper - and *voila*!

If you are interested in my next Imagined-Told-Written story cycle, keep up with me as I write *The Boy from the Top of the Mountain*, in which I attempt to resolve some questions from this story, and send Rani and his loveable cousin on a quest to rescue his long-lost mother. You can follow me at www.annevanroon.com.

CPSIA information can be obtained
at www.ICGtesting.com
Printed in the USA
LVHW04s0509150718
583798LV00002B/2/P